O9-BHK-366

BOW-WOW BIRTHDAY

BY LEE WARDLAW

ILLUSTRATED BY ARDEN JOHNSON-PETROV

BOYDS MILLS PRESS

Published by Caroline House
Boyds Mills Press, Inc.
A Highlights Company
815 Church Street
Honesdale, Pennsylvania 18431
Printed in China

Publisher Cataloging-in-Publication Data
Wardlaw, Lee.
Bow wow birthday / by Lee Wardlaw ; illustrated by Arden Johnson.—1st ed.
[32]p. : col.ill. ; cm.
Summary : A young girl throws a birthday party for her dog and invites her friends from the neighborhood.
ISBN 1-56397-489-4
1. Birthdays—Fiction—Juvenile literature. 2. Dogs—Fiction—Juvenile literature. [1. Birthdays—Fiction. 2. Dogs—Fiction.] I. Johnson, Arden, ill. II. Title.
[E]—dc20   1998   AC   CIP
Library of Congress Catalog Card Number 97-72044

First edition, 1998
Book designed by Abby Kagan
The text of this book is set in 14/17pt Sabon
The illustrations are done in pastels

10 9 8 7 6 5 4 3 2

To Janet Reed Koed,
with fond memories of Rambler
and the dog party
                                    —L. W.
To my friend Marissa
                                    —A.J. P.

Thump. *Tip-tump.*
Maris heard the noise coming from her closet.
She crept to the door and peeked inside.

Rambler, Grandpa's dog, lay curled on the floor, his grizzled snout nuzzling a bunny slipper.

"*Rambler.*" Maris tugged away her slipper. "Come out of there."

Rambler's tail went *Thump. Tip-tump.* Then he shambled after her to breakfast.

"I found Rambler in my closet," Maris said.

"When your bones are old and tired," Mama told her, "sometimes you want to rest where it feels safe and warm."

"Is that why Grandpa went to Florida on vacation?" Maris asked.

Mama laughed. "That's right."

Maris stroked the dog's head. "Are Rambler's bones as old as Grandpa's?"

"Older. Come Saturday, I figure he's . . ." Mama counted on her fingers. "Oh, about a hundred."

"A hundred!"

"In dog years," Mama said with a smile.

"Let's give him a birthday party!" Maris suggested.

"That's a fine idea," said Mama.

After breakfast, Maris found crayons and colored paper to make the invitations.

WOOF WOOF!

Rambler Invites You to His Birthday Party
He's 100 Dog-Years Old!

Saturday at four o'clock
at the home of Rambler's faithful servant,
Maris

P.S. Please wear your favorite dog clothes.

On Saturday, Maris decorated the house. Then she and Rambler had their baths.

After lunch, Maris changed into the paw-print skirt and dog-bone earrings Mama had bought for her at Poppy's Poodle Palace.

Maris raced outside to show Rambler her outfit. "How do I look?"

Rambler yawned. He made two slow circles, then curled in a patch of sun, until it was time to go back inside.

"**R**am-bler. You're crushing your bow!"
Rambler sighed and closed his eyes.
Ding-dong.

"They're here!" Maris sang. She flung open the front door.
Jacob wore floppy ears and a bone bow tie. "I ran all the
way," he said, panting. "A dog catcher is hounding me.
Hounding me. Ha-ha! Get it?"

"I get it," said Maris.

Rosie arrived wearing a thick leather collar with spikes.
"Hi, Rosie," Maris said.
"*Grrrrrrrrrrr,*" answered Rosie.
Isaac wore a dinosaur T-shirt.
"Where are your dog clothes?" Maris demanded.
"I don't like dogs," Isaac said. "I like dinosaurs."
"Oh," said Maris. "Well, it's time to get our dog tags."

She led everyone to the kitchen, where Mama waited with four tags. Each tag dangled from a bright red ribbon.

Mama held up an electric engraving pen. "Name, please."

"Lassie," said Maris.

"Fido," said Jacob.

"Fang," snarled Rosie.

"My name," Isaac announced, "is Tyrannosaurus Rex."

"**Y**ou have to pick a dog name," Maris said. "Like Bowser, or Spot, or Fifi."

Isaac glared at her. *"Tyrannosaurus Rex."*

Maris glared back. "That's *not* a dog name. And it won't fit on the tag."

"Would you like me to bite him for you?" Rosie growled.

"What if we shorten your name to . . . Rex?" suggested Maris.

"Well . . . okay," said Isaac.

Rosie gnashed her teeth. "If you change your mind," she whispered to Maris, "I can bite him later."

Maris led her friends outside to meet the guest of honor.

"This is Rambler," she said.

"What's the matter with him?" asked Isaac. "Is he dead?"

Rambler peered up at Isaac with one eye, then closed it again.

"His bones are tired," Maris said. "He's one hundred years old, you know."

"Sit!" Isaac ordered. "Fetch! Roll over! Speak!"

Rambler sighed.

"Maybe you should change his name to Snoozer," Rosie grumbled.

"Make no bones about it," said Jacob. "He looks dog-eared. *Dog-eared*. Ha-ha! Get it?"

"I get it," Maris said. "Now it's time for the barking contest."

Maris stood atop a small grassy mound. "I'll go first to show everyone how. *Arf-arf-arf! Wook-warf! Wark! Ark-ark-arp!*"

Everyone clapped.

"I'm next," insisted Jacob. He cleared his throat.

"*Yip! Yup! Yawlp! Cock-a-doodle-Woof! Wulf-Warp-Wup.*"

He bowed and sat down.

"**Y**our turn, Isaac," Maris said.

"Tyrannosaurs never bark," said Isaac. "We might roar. We might tear you from limb to limb with a gnash of our razor-sharp teeth. But we *never* bark."

"*Isaac—*"

"I could bite him now, if you like," rumbled Rosie. "That would get a yowl out of him."

"Isaac, you're ruining my party!" Maris cried.

"Oh, all right," said Isaac. "*Bow. Wow.*"

"You're barking up the wrong tree, Isaac," said Jacob. "*Barking up the wrong tree. Get it—?*"

"**R**osie's turn," Maris interrupted.
Rosie hunkered down on all fours. She raised her nose to the sky and closed her eyes.

"*AH-ROOOOOO! AH-ROOOOOO! ARH-ARH-AHROOOOOOOOOOOOOOOOOOOOOOOOOOO!*"

Other dogs in the neighborhood answered with yips, yelps, and howls.

"I'll be doggone," Jacob said.

"Rosie wins," said Maris, handing her a T-shirt that read: IT'S A DOG'S LIFE.

"Who's ready to eat?" asked Maris. "We've got hot dogs, potato salad, carrot sticks, and punch."

"I want cake," Isaac said.

"I thought tyrannosaurs were strictly meat eaters," Maris said.

"Meat *and* cake eaters," said Isaac. With one bite, he chomped his hot dog in half.

"It's a dog-eat-dog world," Jacob said. He piled his plate with food. "Say, Maris, you're really *puttin' on the dog!* Could I get a *doggie bag* for this stuff?"

"Somebody muzzle him," Rosie snarled.

Jacob laughed. "Muzzle! Ha-ha! That's pretty good!"

"I'll get the cake," said Maris.

She hurried inside. Mama helped her light the candles. Very carefully, Maris carried the cake out to the patio, singing "Happy Birthday."

Everyone joined in.

"Happy Birthday, dear Ram-bler . . ."

"Hey," said Maris. "Where *is* Rambler?"

"He was sleeping under that tree," Isaac said.

"That was hours ago," said Maris.

"A dog's age," agreed Jacob. "Ha-ha! Get it?"

"It's not funny," Maris said. "Rambler's missing. We've got to look for him. Rambler! Time for cake! Here, boy!"

"We tyrannosaurs never come when we're called," Isaac said. "It's beneath our dignity."

"I'll bite you in the dignity," Rosie grouched, "if you don't help us look."

"**R**am-bler!"
They searched in the bushes.
"Here, boy!"
They searched behind the woodpile.
"C'mon, Rambler! Come, boy!"

They searched under lounge chairs and the back stairs and the tarp in the toolshed.

"It's getting dark," said Maris.

"We'll find him," Rosie soothed.

"But what if he got out the gate? He doesn't know the neighborhood. He'll get lost."

"He can't go too far," Jacob said. "His bones are tired, remember?"

Maris didn't answer. Instead, she ran to her room.

"**R**ambler?"
She tiptoed to the closet, edged open the door, and peeked inside.
Rambler lay curled on the floor. He opened one eye and peered up at her.
Maris knelt and stroked his head. "Look, Rambler, I have a present for you."
She gave him her bunny slipper. He nuzzled it with his snout.
"Happy Birthday, Rambler," Maris whispered.
Rambler's tail went *Thump. Tip-tump. Thump. Tip-tump.*